ORCA
YOUNG
READERS

Going Places

FRAN HURCOMB

ORCA BOOK PUBLISHERS

Library and Archives Canada Cataloguing in Publication

Hurcomb, Fran, 1949-
Going places / written by Fran Hurcomb.

(Orca young readers)
ISBN 978-1-55469-019-0

I. Title. II. Series.

PS8565.U72G63 2008   jC813'.54   C2008-903059-1

First published in the United States, 2008
Library of Congress Control Number: 2008928574

Summary: Girls' hockey has finally come to Fort Desperation,
Northwest Territories, along with vandalism,
a mystery and the possibility of a road trip.

The author would like to acknowledge the support
of the Northwest Territories Arts Council.

Orca Book Publishers gratefully acknowledges the support for its publishing programs
provided by the following agencies: the Government of Canada through the Book
Publishing Industry Development Program and the Canada Council for the Arts,
and the Province of British Columbia through the
BC Arts Council and the Book Publishing Tax Credit.

Cover artwork by Gary Alphonso
Author photo by Kathleen Smith

ORCA BOOK PUBLISHERS
PO BOX 5626, STN. B
VICTORIA, BC CANADA
V8R 6S4

ORCA BOOK PUBLISHERS
PO BOX 468
CUSTER, WA USA
98240-0468

www.orcabook.com
Printed and bound in Canada.

11 10 09 08 • 4 3 2 1

To all of the Hockey Girls
across the North.

Acknowledgments

Thanks as always to Dave and Kathleen for being supportive and helpful with technical details. Thanks also to Ann Westlake for early editing and encouragement and Sarah Harvey of Orca Book Publishers for her skillful editing, which managed to be both educational and enjoyable.

Chapter One

With four seconds left in the final game, Hayley Wickenheiser scored for Canada on an empty net, and that was it. Game over. Canada had beaten the United States 2–0 to win the Four Nations Cup.

"Wow," said my mom, "what a game."

"Yeah," I replied, relaxing back into the couch in the corner of our café. "They are so good. How can they play like that?"

Mom reached up and turned off the TV; then she settled down on her stool behind the counter. She's the proud owner and proprietor of Casey's Café, the only restaurant in all of beautiful Fort Desperation, Northwest Territories. Casey was my dad, whose dream the whole thing was, way back in the eighties.

He died three years ago, and Mom decided to keep the place going. I am the number-one assistant, which means waitress, dishwasher and cleaning lady, when required.

"Years of practice, Jess. Who knows? Maybe someday you'll play for Team Canada."

I laughed. "Yeah, right. You know what I like best? I like the way they pass the puck around. Way more than in men's hockey."

"I like that there's no bodychecking," added Mom. "I hate seeing men being pounded into the boards. This is much more civilized."

I leaned further back into the couch. "I wonder what it would be like to play girls' hockey?" I said.

"Do you think you'd like it?" asked Mom.

"I don't know, but sometimes I get tired of the boys. Some of them are getting awfully big and mean."

"Well," she said, "I was talking with Milly Smithers...you know, the wife of that new RCMP corporal. They have three girls who all played girls' hockey back in Newfoundland." I'd seen the girls at school. One of them, the middle girl, Daisy, was in my class. Our school is small—a total of about two hundred students from grade one to twelve—

so new faces really stand out. Daisy and her sisters were the topic of many conversations. They seemed friendly, but they kept to themselves. Having an RCMP dad probably meant they had more rules to follow than most of the kids in Fort Desperation.

"Just because it happens in Newfoundland doesn't automatically mean that it will happen here, Mom," I pointed out. "This is the Northwest Territories. We're, like, thirty-five years behind the rest of the country in everything, including girls' hockey."

"Now you know that's not true. We do have the Internet now." She did have a point. The Internet had arrived in Fort Desperation two years ago. It was slow, but it was here.

"Anyway," she continued, "if you'd like, I could do a little research online. I think Yellowknife has girls' hockey now."

"Mom, Yellowknife is big. They even have a Wal-Mart. We have George's Trading Post and Video Rentals. It's just not the same. You can't compare us to Yellowknife."

"Honey, couldn't you try to keep an open mind for a few days? Ask around. You never know. There might be some other girls who'd be interested. Playing with girls might actually be fun, and besides, you're less likely to get hurt."

Ahaaaa...there it was...the real reason for this sudden interest in girls' hockey. Last year I'd broken my collarbone in a boy's game against Hay River. That Melvin Laroque plays so dirty. I never even saw him coming. He flattened me into the boards and skated away with a big grin on his face. They took me off on a stretcher. It was so embarrassing. It made me feel a little better to hear that my teammate Michael Greyeyes beat him up after the game. But still...I was out for the rest of the season, and that sucked.

Boys' hockey was rough, but I was used to it. The boys in town try not to kill me and the other girls, but in the last year or so some of them have grown so much that it even hurts when they lean on me in the corners. I sometimes feel like I'm surrounded by giant aliens. Boys from other communities aren't always so nice. In fact, it sometimes feels like they're out to get the girls, just to let us know that they think we shouldn't be playing hockey.

"Mom, girls' hockey might be totally wimpy. They don't even allow bodychecking. It would be..." I tried to think of the right word. "Dainty!" I said finally.

She laughed. "I can't imagine you or Sam or Geraldine ever being dainty, dear. Sorry. Anyway, think about it a bit and talk to the others. You never know, it might work."

Chapter Two

As I walked down the main road after school the next day, trying hard not to break my ankles in the frozen ruts, I did think about girls' hockey. In some ways, it seemed like a good idea…to have other girls to change with would certainly be more fun. Right now, we had to change in the bathroom off the lobby, one at a time, while the boys got to monopolize the two changing rooms. And I had to admit that even though I had been playing with these boys since I was seven and knew them inside out, I really didn't feel like I belonged with them anymore. Some of them would be quite happy if girls never played.

This year I was supposed to play Bantam. I have one of those end-of-the-year birthdays that always leaves me younger than everyone else on the team. My parents let me stay home an extra year when I was kindergarten age, so I started school later. It works out okay. I'm actually one of the oldest in my grade seven class, which might be why I get good marks.

Bantam was going to be tough. Some of those boys are really big, and they love bodychecking. It seems like that's their favorite part of hockey.

But nothing would ever make me quit hockey. It was the biggest thing in my life. I missed it when the season was finished, and I started dreaming about playing in July or so. In October, a gray time of year in Fort Desperation, the thought of it was all that kept me going. Since we had natural ice in the arena, we wouldn't be playing indoors till almost Christmas, but the pond behind the school would be frozen any day now, so at least there'd be a chance to play outside until the arena was ready.

When I got home, Spider, my skinny, long-legged, totally loveable dog was bouncing up and down on his chain beside the woodpile. His ice-blue eyes were fastened on me, pleading for a walk. "Just a sec, boy. Let me grab your leash, and we'll go," I said.

Spider is great. He's a reject from the sled-dog racing scene. He runs like the wind, but not when he's in harness. Show him a harness, and he goes on strike. One of the dog mushers from down south gave him to me last year after our local race. I was his last chance, and he knew it.

I unclipped him and let him run loose. There wasn't much traffic this time of day. There was never much traffic, come to think of it. We headed to the riverbank, where, with any luck, he might scare up a rabbit for a chase. I liked walking along the riverbank. It was sort of restful, but also interesting. The river was always changing.

The Mackenzie River is the whole reason for Fort Desperation being here at all. Fort Desperation isn't nearly as bad as it sounds. I think that the fur traders who founded it almost two hundred years ago were starving to death or something when they named it. But things must have improved, because it's still here today. About eight hundred people live here now, people of every kind. Lots are Dene or Metis, like me. Some are descendents of the original fur traders.

But there are also people from all over Canada. There are families from China, India and Europe and even a few old draft dodgers from the United States. Mostly everyone gets along okay.

The river looked ominous in the fall gloom. A dusting of snow along the shore only made the swift waters look blacker than ever. Hard to believe that in a month or so it would be frozen almost solid. The days were already getting really short. Soon it would be pitch black when I walked to school in the morning and black again an hour after I got home. We were due for our first blizzard too, and all of the boys were totally hyped for snow. For them, it meant only one thing: snowmobiles. They'd be racing everywhere, day and night.

"Hey." From behind me a familiar voice broke the silence. It was Michael Greyeyes, from my hockey team.

"Hey, yourself," I said.

"How's it going?"

"Not bad." There was a long pause while Michael fell in step beside me. I hadn't seen him much since hockey ended last spring. He had been away for most of the summer, and he's a grade ahead of me at school.

Like the rest of the boys, he had grown lots. He towered over me now. "Going to play this year?" he asked.

"Sure. I mean, what else would I do?"

"Yeah. I heard they were going to try and get the ice in earlier this year, so we can actually start before Christmas."

"That would be cool."

"Yeah." There was another long pause. "The pond is starting to freeze. There might be a game on the weekend if the ice is good. Want to play?" he asked.

"Sure. Guess I should dig out my skates and get them sharpened." There was an old sharpening machine at the gas station where we could sharpen our skates for a dollar apiece. "I hope the machine is still working."

"Yeah. It would be a real drag if it broke. Well… See ya." And with that, he was gone, jogging slowly across the road and heading toward home. I whistled for Spider, who had been happily searching the riverbank for disgusting things to roll in. Luckily, he hadn't found anything. Trying to give Spider a bath was not much fun.

Chapter Three

At school the next day, I had a chance to talk to my two best friends, Sam and Geraldine. We had all started playing hockey together when we were little. We were actually the first girls in Fort Desperation to play hockey, so we got to be a bit famous. My dad was our first coach, and he made it lots of fun, but I think if it hadn't been for Sam and Ger I probably would have given up when the boys started laughing at the way I skated. We stuck it out though, and it was worth it. Last year we played together on a line on the Peewee team and scored a lot of goals.

"What would you think of starting a girls' hockey team?" I asked casually at lunchtime. There was a stunned silence.

"A what?" said Ger.

"A girls' hockey team. You know. No guys, just girls."

"Why would we do that?" asked Sam.

"Well, maybe if all the girls who already play got together, and we could find a few others who'd like to try it out, then we'd have a team. I guess we could practice and then maybe go somewhere for a tournament or something. My mom said she'd look into it if we're interested."

"What a weird idea," replied Ger.

"My mom was talking to the new RCMP corporal's wife. I guess those Smithers girls played girls' hockey in Newfoundland."

"They don't look like hockey players. They look like Barbie dolls," exclaimed Sam.

"They're not that bad. In fact, they're really mean soccer players. I saw them playing at the field when they first got here. They know what they're doing."

"Okay, so say they can actually play. That makes six of us. That's not enough," piped up Geraldine.

"Yeah, I know. I suppose if we could find a few more girls who could skate, we could at least try it out. It would be cool to do a road trip without the boys."

Road trips with the boys were not always fun. They had farting contests and peeing competitions and only wanted to watch gory combat movies on the bus. And they sure didn't want to go to the mall to shop. A road trip with girls would be awesome.

"Maybe we could go to Yellowknife. They have girls' teams there…and a Wal-Mart, and McDonald's and a swimming pool. Yeah, that would be cool," said Geraldine after thinking for a few seconds.

"Yeah. Well, I guess we could ask around a bit. But I'm not going to quit boys' hockey," I said.

"Oh, for sure. I'm not quitting real hockey. This is just for a road trip," agreed Sam.

The one place that everyone in Fort Desperation always goes is George's Trading Post and Video Rentals, known simply as George's. Even if you don't need groceries, you'll probably want to rent a movie sometime. In the lobby is a beat-up bulletin board, which is the main communication center in town. It is plastered with notices for babysitters, firewood, sled dogs for sale, Ski-Doo parts and church bazaars. It was the perfect place to put up the small sign that read: *Are you interested in playing on a girls' hockey team? Contact Mary Middleton at Casey's.* Since Mom wanted to help, I figured this would be a good way to start.

———————

At breakfast a few days later, Mom looked at me with questions in her eyes. "I got a phone call last night from Jewel Graham. She says the twins are interested in playing hockey. Do you know anything about this?"

"Oh no...not the twins." My worst nightmare had come true. Opal and Ruby Graham were twin figure skaters. They had learned a bit about figure skating in Hay River when they were little and could often be seen twirling and leaping in the arena, wasting perfectly good ice time. They wore tiny dresses and gleaming white figure skates. They were definitely not hockey players. "They can't join, Mom. No way."

"What I'd like to know is why they phoned me about it? What does this have to do with me?"

"Well, Mom, you wanted to help. I thought we could use your expertise in organization to get started,"

I replied, trying the old "You slide further on grease than sandpaper" approach.

She glared. "You don't think I'm busy enough running this place fourteen hours a day?"

"Don't worry. Nothing will really happen. There's no way we'll ever get enough players for a team. And the twins are banned!"

Chapter Four

How could I have known that there were so many girls who wanted to play hockey? By Friday, Mom had received four more phone calls, and I had several other inquiries at school. There appeared to be about fifteen girls in town who wanted to play hockey. Yikes!

"Well, now what do we do?" Mom asked Sam, Geraldine and me when we stopped in at the café after school. "Are you girls really into this, or was it just a joke?"

We looked at each other. What did we want to do?

"Well," I said, after a short silence, "what we really want is to go on a road trip, with girls, not boys. But I don't know what to do next." Geraldine and Sam nodded in agreement.

"Next. Yes, next is always a problem," said Mom. There was a long pause while she thought. "I think we need a meeting. That's always safe. We can hope that nobody shows up."

"Yeah, cool. A meeting. I'll make another sign," volunteered Sam.

"We could have it here, Mom, some evening. There's lots of room."

"Okay," agreed Mom, "but I'm not doing any phoning. I draw the line at phoning."

So, Sam made the sign. This one was bigger and fancier, with hockey graphics and colored printing. It let Fort Desperation know that *A meeting for everyone interested in girls' hockey (parents welcome) is being held at Casey's Café on Monday evening at 7 PM.* That would give us the weekend to decide what we really wanted.

Saturday morning dawned clear and cold. Winter was finally here. I scraped a hole in the new frost on the kitchen window. Time to put up the plastic. I peered through the tiny hole and read the thermometer:

minus twenty-two degrees Celsius. All right! It was cold enough to make ice! Lots of ice!

Before I did anything else, I hauled in a few armloads of dry wood and kindling. The woodstove in the café had been sitting patiently, waiting for winter, and this was officially it. I opened the door, stuffed in some paper and kindling and struck a match. I watched while the paper and then the kindling burst into flame. Once it was going well, I added a few small logs and adjusted the damper. For the next six or seven months, the fire would rarely go out. We had an oil furnace, but wood was a lot cheaper. Once it got cold, the woodstove became our main source of heat, and another job for me. At least I didn't have to cut the wood. Once a month, Edward Mercredi delivered a cord to our back door. Six cords got us through most winters.

This is the time of year when I start thinking about my dad a lot. He loved the fall. He said he liked getting ready for winter. Things like cutting firewood, winterizing the house and hunting were fun for him. That's how he died: hunting. He and his best friend Stanley were back in the bush at Lonesome Lake hunting ducks. Stanley's shotgun went off accidentally, and Dad was hit. He died right away. It was the worst time of my life. Mom's too. It's been three years now. That sounds like a long time, but in some ways, it seems like yesterday. So, even though I'm excited in the fall because it's almost hockey season, I'm sad too. I guess I always will be.

After breakfast, I dug through the shed to find my warm boots and my skates. The big question was, would they still fit? I hoped that my feet had finally stopped growing and would stay at size seven. Big enough. The skates were old favorites, given to me by one of my cousins when he outgrew them. When I first got them, they were way too big, but by last year, I had finally grown into them. They were basic black CCMs, but I loved them. Slipping my feet into them was like putting on a soft pair of old jeans; they just felt right. Mom had bought me fluorescent green shoe-laces in Yellowknife last year, so they were downright fancy now. Even though they were still frozen inside, I couldn't wait to try them on. They fit, but just barely. If I wore thin socks, I'd be okay, at least for now. As my mom says, ACP: Another Crisis Past.

I retaped my old stick, put on the warmest clothes that were handy and headed to the pond to see how the ice was. Four other kids were there already, staring at the solid surface of the small pond. It definitely had ice on it.

"Is it any good?" I asked Arvin, the oldest of the kids contemplating the ice.

"Dunno. Joey went home to get an axe."

We waited in silence for Joey to return. It was a yearly ritual, checking the ice. There had to be at least four inches of clear ice before we could skate. The RCMP would be along shortly with axes too, just to make sure we weren't cheating on our measurement.

Joey Lafferty, who played on the Bantam team, returned quickly and casually walked out onto the smooth ice. About two yards from shore he stopped and started chopping. We all held our breath. After about six or so good chops, he was through to water. He put down the axe and stuck his bare hand into the rising water, grasping the top and bottom of the ice to measure its thickness. About four inches! Not bad. He walked out farther onto the pond and repeated the process several more times until he was in the middle, about fifty yards from shore. Last hole. He knelt down and measured again. He stood up with a grin, shook the water off his hand and put it back into his glove.

"It's good," he announced as he strolled back off the ice.

All right! I ran home, grabbed my skates and headed to Dave's Gas Bar to use the skate sharpener before everyone else got the same idea. Hockey season was here.

Hours later the sun slipped below the trees with a golden glow, and the skaters reluctantly straggled home. I sat on a stump trying to pry my skates off my frozen feet. I couldn't even feel them. My ears and fingertips were burning and my knees felt like they were covered in bruises. It had been a great day. Over the course of the afternoon, most of the community had come by just to watch for a few minutes, or to lace up their ancient skates and go for a spin. This was the best time. With no snow to shovel, and good cold weather to make lots of ice, it was like a magical gift. Although the ice surface was covered in cuts and grooves from all the skates, a good wind would polish it and leave it looking brand-new. It was perfect! What we all hoped for was that the snow would hold off for a while.

This would be our only rink for the next month or more, and nobody likes shoveling snow.

I had started skating on this pond when I was three, and it felt like home. Without skating and hockey, my life here would be boring and empty and sad. There really wasn't a lot to do in Fort Desperation, especially for someone my age. If you didn't do sports, most of the options were illegal and downright unhealthy. Winter was my favorite time of year, which was lucky considering it lasted over six months. I wedged my frozen feet into my frozen boots and jumped up and down. Time to get home and check out the damage. Frostbite was always a possibility. Whatever. Tomorrow would be another great day, frostbite or not.

Sure enough, Sunday was another beautiful, clear, cold day. The word was definitely out. Everybody was there, from toddlers to old Mr. and Mrs. St. Germaine, who skated around the edge of the pond, holding hands. They were so cute with their matching beaver-fur hats and mitts. Our hockey game had to tone it down quite a bit to avoid running over the other skaters.

Sam and Geraldine and I took a break and looked around. Daisy, Michelle and Fancy Smithers had just arrived and were lacing up. They looked sort of nervous, which wasn't too surprising, since they were just about the only ones here who hadn't done this every year since they could walk.

"Well, let's just see how good they really are," said Sam, kind of smugly. She obviously wasn't expecting too much. Fancy, the youngest, who was about ten or so, was the first to hit the ice. She stood quietly for a moment and then took off, slowly at first. She quickly built up speed and then, with no warning, she slammed on the brakes, spun and roared back toward her sisters. She slammed on the brakes again, sending a shower of ice into their faces. With a laugh she took off, with both of the older girls in close pursuit. They could skate! In fact, they could really skate. People stopped mid-stride and watched as the girls flew around the ice. Forward, backward, it really didn't seem to matter. They were good!

"Whoa! They're not bad," said Geraldine. "I wasn't really expecting that."

"They probably can't stickhandle," added Sam, a bit miffed that she appeared to be wrong about them.

Personally, I had the feeling that they could probably stickhandle as well as they could skate.

An hour or so later, I screwed up my courage and skated over to the girls, who by now had attracted a large following of boys, all acting crazy and showing off for them.

"Hi, Daisy."

"Hi, Jess. I didn't know you were a hockey player."

"Yeah, I like to play. You too?"

"Yeah, we all do. These are my sisters, Michelle and Fancy."

The Smithers girls were all blond with sparkling blue eyes. Daisy wore glasses, and Fancy had braces. Michelle, who was a year or two older than me, appeared to be perfect. As I looked at them all together, I realized that part of the reason I felt shy around them was that they were so beautiful. I felt like a troll in comparison.

Before I could think of anything intelligent to say, Fancy said, "You're a pretty good skater."

"Thanks. So are you."

Daisy broke into a loud laugh. "Boy, we sure are polite."

We all grinned at once. These girls were okay. If they wanted to play girls' hockey, they could be just what we needed.

"What position do you play?" I finally asked when the laughter died down.

"Well," she replied, "I usually played center at home, but I can play wing too. I really suck at defense."

"Me too. Whenever I play defense, the other team scores right away. Are you going to play here?" I asked.

"I'm not sure what we're going to do here yet. What kind of hockey have you got?"

"Well, we've got the usual minor hockey teams, you know: Atoms, Peewees, Bantams, Midgets, but just one team of each so we usually have to travel to play other teams."

"No girls' teams?" asked Michelle.

"No, there are only a few girls who actually play." I paused, trying to think about how to bring up the meeting. Finally, I just blurted it out. "But we're having a meeting on Monday night at my mom's café, to see if anyone's interested in girls' hockey. You should come."

By now Sam and Geraldine had skated over as well and stood staring at the girls. I introduced them quickly. Smiles were exchanged, and then Daisy continued. "Yeah, that might be cool. We'll ask our parents about it."

"Great. Well, see you later. At school probably. Bye." And off we skated, aware that our every stride was being watched.

Chapter Five

The café was packed. All five tables were full, as was the counter. The café isn't much, really. Once upon a time it had been the priests' residence for the old church school. My Dad bought it from the church and tore out a lot of the inside walls downstairs. He fixed up the upstairs and made us an apartment there, with stairs going up the outside at the back of the building. It may not be fancy, but it's home.

The café itself is kind of plain, but it has matching curtains and tablecloths, old photographs on the walls and good food. A counter with stools runs across the front of the room, separating it from the kitchen. What more does a place like Fort Desperation need? It's pretty popular, and Mom is busy most of the time.

"Coffee's on the house" announced Mom in a loud voice that could barely be heard over the hubbub. We were almost killed in the stampede to the counter. I guess free coffee is hard to find these days.

Sam and Geraldine and I surveyed the situation. The Smithers girls were there, with both parents. Their dad was huge—about six foot six—with regulation short hair and a kind of watchful look about him. Their mom, on the other hand, was tiny. The girls looked a lot like her.

Alyssa and Heather, who played Peewee, were there too, with their parents. The Graham twins, Opal and Ruby, had come with their mom. Two of the Beaulieu girls, who were in grade five and six, were sitting alone in a corner, trying hard to be invisible. I guess when you come from a family as big as theirs, you get used to being invisible. There were several other girls that I recognized but didn't really know, with one or the other of their parents as well. Sitting alone in another corner was our community recreation director, Tara Richardson. She had arrived in the spring and had spent the summer trying to organize baseball and swimming lessons, without much success. So far, I counted fifteen girls, including me, Sam and Ger. This was scary!

Mom cleared her throat really loud, stared at me for a long moment and said, "I guess we should start talking about this hockey thing so we can get done real fast." There were nods of approval, and then everyone just stared at her. Finally, Mrs. Smithers broke the silence.

"What exactly did you have in mind for the girls?" she asked.

Mom looked at me again before answering.

"Well, actually, I didn't have anything in particular in mind at all. I just asked around to see if anyone was interested in girls' hockey, and here we are."

I couldn't stand feeling guilty anymore. I stood up. "My name's Jess, and I've been playing hockey with the boys for five years. So have my friends, Sam and Geraldine." I gestured to them in the hope that they would help me out. They were both busy examining the floorboards.

"We were just thinking it would be fun to have a girls' team in town so that maybe we could travel somewhere to a tournament or something. They have girls' hockey in lots of places now."

"Our girls played in Newfoundland," said Mrs. Smithers. "It was great, wasn't it, girls?" They all nodded in unison. "The town we lived in was small, so all of the girls played on one team, and at the end of the year they traveled to St. John's for a tournament. It was a great trip." She beamed at her audience. Then she sat down. Another dead silence.

Finally a man asked, "What would we need to get going?"

"Well," replied Mom, who actually knew a lot more about hockey than she let on, "a coach would be good. A bit of equipment for those who don't have any would be nice too. Maybe someone to put in a good word for us so that we could get some free ice time."

"Maybe I could be some help there." Everyone turned around to see who was talking. It was Tara Richardson. She smiled in an embarrassed way and continued. "I could talk to the Band Council about free ice time. They'd probably be happy to see something like this getting started. And maybe if we asked around, we could come up with some used equipment that the older kids have outgrown." There were murmurs of agreement from around the room.

"Yeah, but where are we going to find a coach? There's no way Joe can coach any more teams. He's got his hands full now."

Joe was Joe Savage, a teacher at the school. He'd been coaching all four teams since he came here years ago, and he really did have his hands full.

There was a long silence while we all thought about that one. Then, finally, "I've got it," one of the dads said. "Curtis Beaulieu."

Slowly, all the heads in the room nodded and then turned in unison to the back corner, where our eyes locked on the two small Beaulieu girls. They had that wide-eyed look of rabbits caught in the garden.

"What do you think, Sarah?" my mom asked gently. "Would your Uncle Curtis coach?" Sarah, the older of the two, swallowed and then looked at her sister, Lucy, for moral support. Nothing but terror there.

In the quietest voice possible, Sarah finally spoke. "Uncle, he's pretty busy. He works at the diamond mine. And he don't like people much." Her sister nodded. There was another silence while everyone thought about Curtis Beaulieu.

Anyone who'd lived in Fort Desperation for any length of time knew Curtis Beaulieu's story. I'd heard it tons of times. About the time that I was born, Curtis Beaulieu had been the best young hockey player in the North. He moved out to Alberta to play Midget A and finish high school. As soon as he was old enough, he was drafted by the Calgary Flames. To us, and to most northerners, he was a hero—an example of what could happen if you worked hard enough, even if you did live at the end of a gravel road north of absolutely everywhere. And then, only three years into his amazing career, a high stick caught him in the eye and ended his career.

After that the story gets a bit vague, but eventually, he came home. He had totally changed from a happy, outgoing young man into a bitter recluse. It's true that you hardly ever see him in town. I think he works at the mine two weeks in, two weeks out, so that accounts for some of it. Once in a while I see him drive by in a big, new pickup truck. He built a small house on the edge of town, near the riverbank, and in the summer we sometimes see him out in his boat, but he's always alone. We've never seen him play hockey.

Sam's dad, William Blackduck, spoke up. "We used to hang out together, a long time ago. I guess I could try asking him. But I don't know. Like the girls said, he don't like people much no more." Heads nodded in agreement.

"Well," my mom said, "I guess until we get a coach, that's about as far as we can go. I have a piece of paper here, so how about if every girl puts her name and phone number on it, so at least we know who's interested."

The meeting ended. Fourteen girls had signed up—enough for a team. Now all we needed was a coach.

Chapter Six

The week dragged on. Nothing too exciting was happening at school. It was still clear and cold, so the pond was busy after school with lots of skaters. A couple of the dads rigged up a spotlight on a tree and powered it with a generator. About nine o'clock every night, someone's dad would come and shut the generator off, load it into his truck and that would be that, unless there was a full moon.

Thursday night after the generator went home, I was warming up in the café with a hot chocolate when Curtis Beaulieu strolled in. I was so surprised to see him that I just stared. Finally he asked, "Is your mom here?" I didn't even know he knew who we were.

"Sure. I'll go get her."

Mom was in the kitchen shutting things down.

"Curtis Beaulieu is here," I told her. For some reason, I felt I should be whispering. "He wants to talk to you."

"Oh," she said in a strange voice. She dried her hands on a towel, undid her apron and walked out into the front.

"Hi, Curtis. Would you like a coffee?"

"No, thanks," he said. While he stood there, I had a chance to look at him. I had overheard my mom and her friends talking about him one day and saying he was "cute." Maybe he was, for an old guy. He had to be at least thirty.

"William told me about your girls' hockey idea. I just wanted to let you know that I can't coach. I didn't want you to get the wrong idea." He must have read the disappointment on our faces, because he quickly continued. "I'm too busy. I'm at the mine for two weeks every month, so there's no way."

"How about when you're in town?" asked Mom. "All we need is a little help to get started. It wouldn't be much."

His face clouded over, and his eyes narrowed. He probably hadn't expected to have to argue his way out of this. He obviously didn't know my mom.

"No, it's not something I want to do. I'm busy." He stood there for a moment; then he started to turn away.

"Curtis Beaulieu," Mom said in the voice that usually meant I was in trouble. "A lot of people spent a lot of time with you when you were young, to help your dreams come true. You should remember that."

"A lot of good those dreams did me," he replied with a scowl.

Mom paused and looked at him carefully. "I'm sorry about the way things worked out for you, but it's not all bad. You've still got a good education, a good job and the respect of a lot of people. You know, to this town, you're still a hero, NHL or no NHL. So remember that. It wouldn't hurt you to give the girls a hand for a few hours now and again." She was glaring at him now, defying him to answer back. He got a kind of confused look in his eyes, and then he simply turned and left the café.

"Well, I guess I blew that. Oh well, there's bound to be someone else," Mom said, with a long sigh.

"I don't think you blew it, Mom. I think he did."

She gave me a huge hug and said, "Thanks, sweetie."

At school the next day, I told Sam and Geraldine and the Smithers girls about the encounter at the café.

"There must be something that we can do," said Daisy. "There must be someone else in this town who knows about hockey."

"My dad is a real expert on hockey," said Sam. "Only problem is, he can't skate."

"Yeah, I expect there are a lot of those kinds of hockey experts around. We need someone who can actually play the game."

"What if we just went out by ourselves and started playing?" I suggested. "We all know enough to run a few drills and stuff like that. At least that's better than doing nothing."

Everyone nodded in agreement; it was a lot better than doing nothing. We decided that we would each phone two other girls on the list and meet at the pond Saturday morning. We agreed to get to the pond by about ten o'clock, to beat the rush. Everyone was going to bring all the pucks they could find so we could practice all at once. It still hadn't snowed, so at least we didn't have to worry about shoveling. Girls' hockey was about to begin.

By ten fifteen there were nine of us laced up and ready to go. We had the rink all to ourselves. Then the Graham twins arrived—with their figure skates.

"You can't play hockey on those," said Sam with a nasty frown. "You'll trip and kill yourselves."

"It's all we've got," they replied. "We brought sticks though. And a puck."

Michelle got things rolling. "Okay. Three laps around the pond to warm up." Off we went, building up speed as we warmed up. The morning was crisp and cold—about minus twenty—so we had to keep moving if we didn't want to freeze.

Compared to the hockey players, the twins had a funny choppy way of skating, although they could pretty well keep up with everyone. The big surprise came when Michelle shouted out, "Three laps backward." The twins picked up speed and passed everyone with their figure-skating crossovers. It didn't help everyone's mood when Opal launched herself into some sort of fancy jump.

"That's not hockey," screamed Geraldine. "You can't do that in hockey." She smacked her stick on the ice and scowled.

"Sorry," Opal smirked. "I couldn't resist. I won't do it again."

Michelle called everyone over to the middle of the ice. "Okay," she said. "We can all skate. But those figure skates will have to go if you actually want to play hockey. Does anyone have any extra skates at home?"

After a moment, little Sarah Beaulicu piped up. "We got some boxes with hockey stuff in the shed. I think Uncle used to send equipment home for my brothers when he played down south."

"That would be great. Do you think we could look at the stuff?"

"I'll ask my mom. She'd probably be glad to get rid of it."

Before practice was over, two more girls, Denise and Morgan, showed up. They had never played hockey, but they could sort of skate. We certainly had enough bodies for a team, but what did we do next?

By eleven thirty we were cold. The Beaulieu girls agreed to ask their mom about the equipment and to try and bring the boxes to the pond on Sunday. We all agreed to be back at the pond the next morning for our second practice. So far so good. Michelle and I were doing our best to keep the practices going, but we really needed someone who was older and had more experience. It felt good to be out there, anyway.

As we were unlacing, the guys from the Bantam team arrived.

"What's happening?" asked Jasper McKay.

Suddenly I felt embarrassed. They would laugh at the whole idea of a girls' team. "Oh, just, you know, skating," I said as coolly as possible.

"You girls playing hockey?"

"Yeah. Sort of."

"You any good?"

"We will be after we practice for a while," replied Daisy. She looked right at him with a big smile. "We'll challenge you to a game after a few practices."

The boys burst into laughter. Finally, Michael Greyeyes managed to stop laughing long enough to reply, "Okay. It's a date."

And then they were gone. Showing off as usual. Skating as fast as they could and snapping passes back and forth.

"Daisy. Why did you say that?" asked Sam. "They'll kill us."

"Oh well. I just couldn't resist. They're so cocky. It'll give them something to think about anyway."

I felt more embarrassed than ever. I should have been out there with the guys, not practicing with a bunch of girls who hardly knew what they were doing. I must be crazy.

Chapter Seven

The next morning we showed up at the pond and started lacing up. It seemed as though some of our enthusiasm was gone. Even Daisy was quiet. The twins arrived with their figure skates and asked about Sarah and the mysterious boxes in the shed.

"No sign of her yet."

"She probably couldn't find them. You know how sheds are. They're probably way at the back."

"Yeah," replied Daisy, kind of sadly. "I've been thinking about equipment. You know, you need a ton of stuff to start hockey. I mean, we're okay. We brought our stuff with us from Newfoundland, and I expect you have your old stuff, but it will be really expensive to buy new equipment for the girls just starting out."

She gestured to the twins and the three other new girls who were hopping around, trying to keep warm. "Maybe this idea won't work out too well."

I knew what she meant. Most people in Fort Desperation don't have a lot of money to spare for things like hockey equipment.

I looked up at the ring of solemn faces surrounding me. "Well, let's not give up just yet," I said, with more enthusiasm than I felt. "We'll all freeze to death if we don't get moving. Let's go." And we were off, skating around the pond, practicing our stickhandling.

After a few minutes I looked up to see a black pickup truck making its way through the playground toward the pond. It was a new truck, one that I didn't recognize. It stopped right behind the log benches where we changed. Then I saw Sarah waving and smiling. She leapt out of the truck as soon as it stopped and raced over to us.

"I got the stuff," she said, jumping up and down with excitement. "There's lots of it. Mom told Uncle to help me bring it here. Come on!"

We followed her to the edge of the pond, where her Uncle Curtis was unloading box after box of equipment. Five boxes in all! Without saying anything, we tore open the first box. Skates, shin guards, gloves, helmets. It was all there!

We all stood back in amazement and then looked up at Curtis, who still had the last box in his arms. "Dig in, girls," he said with a grin. "This stuff has been sitting in the shed since the boys outgrew it. In fact, some of it looks like it was never used at all."

"Are there any size-six skates in there?"

"Well," he said, "let's take a look." And that was it. Within seconds, there was equipment all over the snow. It was amazing. There were even some old hockey sweaters.

"Was this yours?" I asked him. I was holding up a bright red jersey with a wolf on the front and the number 12 on the back.

He laughed softly, and shook his head slowly. "Wow. I'd forgotten all about that. Yeah, that was my jersey from my first Junior team in Alberta. The Lethbridge Wolves. Boy, that was a long time ago." He smiled and continued to look at the jersey.

"Here are some size sixes," came a voice from the other side of the huddle of girls. "Try these, Opal." Opal sat on the bench and undid her figure skates. She stared at the hockey skates like she had never seen such bizarre things before. Slowly she eased her foot into one skate. A look of complete amazement came over her face.

"I can wiggle my toes," she yelled. "I've never been able to wiggle my toes in skates before!"

Meanwhile her sister, Ruby, was making a similar discovery. They tightened up their new skates and stood up. Skating without picks was going to be a strange experience for them. The rest of us lined up to watch. This was going to be good.

"Here, better put these on, just in case," said Curtis, handing them each a helmet. He helped them snap the helmets on, and they wiggled their heads around trying to get used to the feeling.

"Actually, you should all be wearing your helmets, even out here," said Curtis quietly. We all looked at him and nodded. His eye injury had happened in a practice, when he and his teammates were just fooling around. He didn't have to say anything more. I had brought my helmet along out of habit, but hadn't put it on because there was no coach to tell me to do it. There were more than enough helmets in the boxes, so after some experimenting, we were all set.

Opal and Ruby looked at their new skates, at each other and then at the ice.

"Well, let's go," said Ruby. And she walked out onto the ice. She took two steps and fell to her knees. "Ow. This is going to be hard. Everything feels weird." We all shouted encouragement and tried to explain how to skate on hockey skates. Up and down the twins went. I had to give them credit: They were stubborn.

All of a sudden, a new voice joined in. "Here," said Curtis, who had put on a pair of old skates while we were concentrating on the twins. "Like this," he said pushing his skate to the side with a powerful thrust.

We all stood there, perfectly quiet, and watched while he demonstrated the mechanics of skating in hockey skates to the twins. He made it look so easy.

The next hour was a whirlwind of excitement. The new girls were getting used to wearing equipment, while those of us who had played before helped them with useful suggestions like "Shin guards go under the socks." Turns out there were actually enough old sweaters and socks in the boxes for everyone. A lot of time was spent on color coordination.

"I'm not wearing orange socks with this red jersey," said Opal. "It totally clashes."

Curtis listened to these conversations with a strange look in his eyes. When a taker for the orange socks was finally found (it was Sarah, who was wearing a black jersey with what appeared to be a moose in a Santa costume on the front), he finally burst out laughing.

"You girls are too much." He laughed and shook his head. "How about three final laps around the pond and we'll call it a day." As we took off, I wondered if we might have found our coach.

It felt really good to see everyone dressed in hockey gear. It seemed as though our skating had improved one hundred percent. Even the twins were getting the hang of the hockey skates, although they still moved sort of strangely and spent a lot of time on their knees. When we all skated over to the benches to take our skates off, Sarah quietly spoke up.

"Uncle, are you going to be our coach?"

All conversation stopped, mid-sentence. It was kind of like putting a DVD on pause.

He smiled. "Well, I guess I could if you want me. I—" He couldn't get another word out before Sarah and her little sister Lucy threw themselves on him. A cheer went up from the whole group. We were a team!

Chapter Eight

Curtis drove me home with all of the extra equipment. We'd still have to try on the underneath stuff somewhere warm. He helped me carry the boxes into the café.

"Hmmm," said Mom. "What have we got here?"

"Equipment. Tons of it. Sarah found it in their shed."

Mom looked at Curtis, like she was waiting for more. He smiled and added, "Just a bunch of old stuff I sent home years ago. They tried some of it out. I think it will fit. We need somewhere to leave the rest of it until they can try it on." Curtis smiled at Mom and continued. "I thought about what you said the other day, and you were right. A lot of people did help me out when I was starting. I guess it's my turn. Only problem will be that I'm away half the time. We'll have to find somebody else to help out too."

Mom beamed at Curtis and looked like she might hug him right then and there. No, Mom, no! Luckily she heard my silent plea.

"Well, we'll tackle that problem next. Thanks, Curtis. This is just great. You can leave the boxes over there, under the stairs, and the girls can come here to try stuff on."

Curtis grinned and turned to leave. "Will you girls be there after school tomorrow?"

"Sure," I replied. "I'll let everyone know."

After he was gone, Mom seemed unusually quiet. Instead of peppering me with questions like she usually did, she just stared blankly at the door. Finally, she came back to reality and smiled at me.

"I was pretty sure Curtis would come through. He was always a good guy. Your dad coached him for years, you know. He always knew Curtis had what it took to go places. Your dad was the one who convinced him to try playing hockey down south, and he was devastated when Curtis got hurt. I think he always felt responsible. If he hadn't encouraged Curtis to leave, Curtis would probably still have his sight in both eyes." Mom looked so sad that I just had to hug her. I felt sad too. I missed Dad so much. Three years is a long time to think about someone every day.

"If Dad was still here, I'll bet he would have coached us," I blurted out, as tears filled my eyes. It still hurt to talk about him.

"Yes, I'll bet he would have," replied Mom softly.

Overnight the weather warmed up, and the clouds rolled in. Soon there would be snow. Well, we had been lucky for almost two weeks. Let the shoveling begin.

As I walked to school, Michael Greyeyes fell in step with me.

"Hi."

"Hi." We weren't the greatest conversationalists.

"I hear the Zamboni is broken. They've had to order parts," he said after a while.

"Oh no. Not again!" This seemed to happen every year. It was bad enough that we had to wait until it was cold enough to make natural ice. Now we'd probably miss valuable ice time waiting for parts, yet again.

"How's your team coming?" asked Michael.

"Great. Curtis Beaulieu is going to coach us, at least when he's in town."

"Wow. How did you manage that?"

"Well, his nieces, Sarah and Lucy, are on the team. Plus, my mom kind of guilted him into it."

"So how many players you got?"

"Well," I said, counting in my head, "about fifteen or so that are showing up right now."

"Who's in goal?"

Goal? Good question.

"Nobody so far." We hadn't even thought about that. Without a goalie, we weren't much of a hockey team.

"You know, I was thinking," said Michael. "My sister Alice might give it a try."

Alice Greyeyes? She was famous! She was the best soccer goalie ever. She even made the Arctic Winter Games team last year and went all the way to Alaska to play. She won MVP on the team.

"Can she skate?"

There was a long pause. "Well, not really. You know. She skates a few times every fall on the pond and then a few more times in the arena. I guess she can stand up okay, but I don't think she can move very fast."

"Do you really think she'd be interested?"

"No idea. Why don't you ask her?"

Gulp. Alice was in grade nine. How much time would she have for a bunch of lowly middle schoolers? For that matter, how much time would she have for hockey?

"I guess I could try. But I don't know her."

"Alice won't bite, you know. She's actually okay, for an older sister. She's really into training and stuff, so maybe you could push the fitness angle."

"Okay," I said, very hesitantly. "I guess I could try."

We walked through the school's front doors and into the colorful chaos that was Chief Hardisty School. If I was going to talk to Alice, I was going to need backup. Notes were passed, and at lunchtime, the entire team met in the lunchroom.

"So I had this idea. Well, actually, Michael Greyeyes had this idea. He thinks that maybe his sister, Alice, would play goal for us." Stunned silence. It was almost too much to consider.

"But does she know anything about hockey? Can she skate? Why would she do that?" Questions flew around the group.

Finally I took the lead. "Well, we could at least ask her, I suppose. She can only say no."

"Yeah," came the group reply.

"When are we going to do this?" asked Opal.

"Well," said Sam, who was braver than the rest of us, "we're all here now. Let's go find her." Off we marched, down the halls to the gym, where we hoped she'd be hanging out.

All fifteen of us tried to march through the gym doors at once, so our mission began to look like some kind of slapstick comedy. We finally stumbled through the doors and into the gym. There she was, with her soccer team, kicking a ball around. Everything ground to a halt while we stood there, staring. Finally, one of the other soccer players said, "Yeah?" and Sam, our fearless spokesperson, sprang into action.

"Alice, could we talk to you for a second?" Alice looked up, staring. She looked a lot like Michael, except prettier. She bounced a soccer ball off her knee. "Me? Why?"

"Uh, we, uh, just, uh…" Sam suddenly seemed at a loss for words. We all stood there, afraid to open our mouths. After what seemed like an hour, Sam tried again. "We're, uh, the girls' hockey team. We, uh, don't have a goalie. We thought maybe you'd like to try it out. You wanna be our goalie?" She smiled a sickly smile and held her breath.

Alice looked at us like we were all crazy. "Me? I can't play hockey. I can barely skate. Can't you find a real goalie? I mean, why me?"

Another silence. And then Sarah's small voice piped up from the back. "Because you're the best, and we need the best." Alice burst out laughing.

"Are you that bad?"

"Yes," replied Sam, "but we have potential. And maybe we can go on a road trip." Ahhhh, the magic words. I sometimes think if it weren't for road trips, most of us wouldn't actually bother with organized sports. But that's one of the good things about living far away from absolutely everything...any road trip is just about guaranteed to be a good one. Even Hay River, population three thousand, sounds exciting to kids like us, living without so much as a movie theater in their community.

"But...okay, I'll have to think about it. But I warn you, I can't skate. I'll probably have to be propped up. Do you have any equipment?" We all started to talk at once. Somebody's brother had this, someone else's had that.

"We'll come up with equipment if you'll just come out once or twice and try it out. We promise not to bug you if you decide not to do it after that," said Sam. She was certainly sounding grown-up all of a sudden.

"Well, okay," agreed Alice, still shaking her head in surprise. "I'll try anything once."

Alice agreed to meet us after school two days later. We had two days to find equipment.

The snow started about 1:00 PM. Big gentle flakes drifted down from the heavy gray sky. It was beautiful. Without snow, winter just didn't feel right. It would be at least six months before we saw the ground again. This made me a little sad, but the beauty of it all quickly erased any sad thoughts from my brain. Of course, now we'd have to start shoveling the rink. This would really separate the hockey players from the couch potatoes.

Chapter Nine

Sure enough, the snow came down…and down…and down. The snowmobilers in town were thrilled. You were taking your life in your hands walking down the street. It sometimes seemed as though every crazy teenager in town had the use of a very hot snow machine. They went roaring up and down the streets and trails until about midnight. Of course, people complained about it nonstop, but it was hard to do anything about them because they were too fast for the bylaw officers to catch. Besides that, they were all dressed like Darth Vader, with black plastic helmets, black visors and black clothing. Everyone looked exactly the same.

My mom says that when snowmobiles first arrived in Fort Desperation they were really useful.

They replaced dog teams as the best type of winter transportation. They were great for hauling wood, breaking trail and generally getting trappers and hunters around in the bush. Now they're basically just very expensive toys, and I don't like them. Too noisy and smelly. Too dangerous.

Anyway, it was snowing so heavily that we had to take a day off practice. There was no way we could ever shovel fast enough to keep ahead of the snow. That was actually a good thing, because it gave us time to get our equipment organized. The girls all came to the café, and we got everybody sorted out with equipment. We also got a few donations from older brothers. The biggest surprise came from the Graham twins, who staggered into the café dragging a huge duffel bag.

"What have you got in there, a body?" asked Sam.

"You'll never believe this," said Ruby. "Our dimwit brother was once a goalie!" And with that, they dumped a pile of equipment onto the floor. The smell was awful, but it looked like everything a goalie would ever need was there.

My mom's customers were getting used to the café being hockey central. Some of them had been quite useful in helping us figure out which bits of equipment were which. Black Mike, an old truck driver who wasn't even black, looked at our goalie gear. "Boy, this stuff is old. Looks like something I might have wore."

"You were a goalie? No way," said Sam with her usual tact.

"Sure. Back in Yellowknife, years ago. Played for the Giant Grizzlies. Course we didn't use helmets, them days. Or a face mask. Sissy stuff. See this scar?" He pointed to a nasty-looking scar that cut one eyebrow in half. "Slapshot. Game against Con. Played the whole last period with my eye swole right shut." He grinned a mainly toothless grin, chuckled and went back to his coffee. Sarah and the twins pulled faces when his back was turned. Black Mike was a café regular, so I was used to him, but I guess other people thought he was a bit weird.

While we surveyed the pile, the door opened again and out of the whirling snow came Tara, the rec coordinator.

"Wow," she said, brushing off her hood and clapping her mitts free of snow. "Some storm." She came over to admire our pile of stuff. "Where did you get all of this?" she asked, obviously impressed.

"Oh, here and there," replied Sam, attempting to be cool.

We didn't really know Tara very well yet. She had moved to Fort Desperation in the spring and had worked hard all summer to keep us kids occupied and out of trouble. She organized baseball tournaments, swimming lessons and soccer clinics. There were camping trips, canoeing lessons and craft nights. There was only one problem. In the summer, northerners, kids especially, like to stay up half the night and sleep half the day. Since it's light all the time, it doesn't really matter when you sleep, so anything that's scheduled or organized doesn't work very well. The summer is our free time after a long dark winter, and we're sure not going to ruin it with lessons!

Winter, however, is another thing. The days are short and the cold is sometimes really extreme. Of course, from my point of view, the whole reason for winter is to play hockey, so once the arena is operating, cold and darkness aren't huge problems.

"Good news about ice time," said Tara. "You'll be able to get ice at least three times a week, just like the boys, once the arena opens. Isn't that great?"

"Yeah. If the arena ever opens," said Geraldine, who was busy trying on shoulder pads.

"Well," replied Tara, "from what I could understand, they've ordered the parts they need for the Zamboni and they should be here next month. Are you girls still practicing on the pond?"

"Yeah, except all of this snow is going to slow things down quite a bit," replied Sam.

"Yes, I suppose it will," said Tara solemnly. Her face suddenly lit up. "Well, I'll see you all later," she said as she hurried out the door.

"Wonder what she's up to?" mused Sam.

"Maybe she's going to start a craft class to make Zamboni parts," Ger giggled. That got a good laugh from everyone as we continued to sort through the smelly bags of equipment.

The snow finally stopped overnight. At lunchtime, we all agreed to bring shovels with us after school. There looked to be about six inches of the fluffy stuff on the ground. This was going to be brutal.

As I walked to the pond after school, the sun was dipping below the trees and the sky glowed pink and blue. In the distance, I could hear a motor. Sounded like a generator or a chainsaw on steroids. As I got closer, I could tell that the sound was coming from the pond. In the distance, I could see a small figure in red. The air over the pond looked thick, like it was in the middle of a snowstorm. I slowly began to see that the small red figure was pushing something back and forth on the pond. A snowblower! Someone was using a snowblower on the pond! I raced down to the edge and dropped my gear. Small stakes had been placed around the edge of the area that was being cleared. There, in the middle of the pond, covered in snow and frost, was Tara. Because of the noise of the machine, she hadn't heard me arrive. Slowly and methodically, she pushed the snowblower down the length of the ice surface that she had marked out. When she reached the end, she paused before turning around. She looked up for a moment, saw me and waved.

"I'm almost done," she called above the roar of the machine. She turned and headed down the far side of the rink. That's what it was—a rink! Our pond had become a real rink. Now it had edges. It looked almost the same size as the rink in the arena. Wow! She must have been at it all day.

I quickly laced up my skates and headed out with my shovel to clear the last little bit of snow off the surface. While I whizzed back and forth with my shovel, the others arrived. They were all as amazed as I was and quickly hit the ice to help. Tara finished the far edge and pushed the machine over to the benches. She shut it off and sat down.

"Whew," she said. "I'm glad that's done. There was a lot of snow." She was covered in snow and frost. Even her eyelashes were heavy with tiny snowballs.

"Yikes," screamed Sam, when she got close enough to see Tara better. "A bushman. Or maybe I should say bushwoman."

Tara growled a not very convincing growl and shook herself. Snow flew all over us. Behind us, a pickup truck pulled up and stopped. Curtis hopped out and strolled over.

"Wow. Now that's a rink," he said. He looked at Tara, trying to see who was under the layers of snow and frost. "Looks like you might be responsible for this," he laughed.

Tara smiled shyly and nodded.

Sam, with her newfound maturity, jumped to the rescue.

"This is Tara, the new rec director," she said to Curtis. "This is Curtis, our coach," she explained to Tara.

Curtis and Tara smiled at each other and then quickly looked away. Weird! Maybe Tara thought Curtis was cute too.

"This is great," said Curtis finally. "Thanks a lot. Saved the girls a lot of shoveling."

"Oh, that's okay," replied Tara. "It was kind of fun. I borrowed the snowblower from the hamlet garage. Might as well put it to good use. I even brought my skates. Do you mind if I take a spin around while you practice?"

"Go ahead," replied Curtis. "I mean, it is your rink!"

Tara laughed. "It's not mine! It's for everyone. That even includes boys," she added with a grin.

"Oh no." We all groaned.

"Oh yes," she said. "It's for anyone who spends a bit of time cleaning it occasionally."

"Fair enough," said Curtis. "Okay, girls, let's get some of that fancy equipment on and we'll run a few drills."

We had just started into our drills when a snow machine with two people on it came roaring across the playground toward us. It braked to a halt by the benches and shut down. The figure on the back took off its helmet. It was Alice Greyeyes! In all the excitement of the new rink, we had completely forgotten that she was coming. The driver, her boyfriend, Cory, removed his helmet as well and scowled at us. Alice walked slowly over to the bench, a pair of skates slung over her shoulder.

"It's Alice," yelled Lucy. "Uncle, our new goalie is here."

Lucy was so excited that she completely wiped out as she raced toward Alice. She slid across the ice on her stomach and stopped right by Alice's feet. "Hi." She grinned.

"Hi, yourself," replied Alice.

"Are you going to put on your equipment?" asked Lucy.

"Well, I don't know quite what I'm supposed to do," replied Alice.

"Oh," said Lucy gravely. "Well, Uncle will know. He's our coach," she said with obvious pride.

On cue Curtis skated over, smiling. "I'm Curtis Beaulieu. I guess I'm the coach. At least for the next few days."

Alice introduced herself. "The girls asked me if I'd try out to be their goalie," she explained.

"Are you usually a goalie?"

"Actually, I'm a soccer goalie. I don't know anything about hockey."

"Oh," said Curtis with a nod. "Well, do you want to give it a try?"

"I guess I could," Alice replied.

"Can you skate?"

"Not very well. I can stand up, but that's about it."

"Okay. Well, why don't you put on your skates and grab a helmet and a stick, and we'll get you skating a bit to start with." Curtis smiled at her, and then he skated back to the center of the rink. "Come on, girls. It's going to be dark soon. Let's get going."

Chapter Ten

The rest of the week passed in a blur: school, hockey, school, hockey. Having Curtis as a coach had given everyone a major lift. He had us doing drills we had never tried before. We were improving every day, especially the new girls. The biggest surprise had to be the twins. They still skated sort of funny, but Curtis had quickly noticed something—they were great going backward. Nobody, not even the Smithers girls, could keep up with them. According to Curtis, they were going to be the core of our defense.

We had lots of forwards. Sam, Ger and I had played together last year on a line, and so had the Smithers girls. Sarah and Alyssa were getting pretty good on defense. Little Lucy was as slippery as a weasel. She seemed to be able to sneak through or around most of us. When she got bigger, she was going to be great. The newer players like Morgan and Denise were still trying out different positions.

Alice was doing okay in goal, as well. She could skate a bit, so standing in net on skates was not going to be a big problem. All those years of playing goal in soccer had given her quick reflexes and an instinct for where a shot was likely to go. For her, it was the equipment that was the problem.

"There's just so much of it," she complained. "It must weigh thirty pounds. And that mask. It's always in the way. I can't see anything." She was totally exasperated. Curtis laughed.

"Well, I know what you mean," he said, "but believe it or not, you'll get used to it. You're strong and fast. You're going to be a great goalie." Alice glowed.

The only thing I was worried about was her boyfriend. I heard at school that Cory was giving her a hard time about playing hockey. Maybe he thought it was taking up too much of her time. I guess it would all boil down to how much she was enjoying it. So far, so good.

After Friday's practice, Curtis called us all together. "Well, tomorrow's the day I head out to camp. I'll be gone for two weeks."

There was a long groan. "What are we going to do?"

"Well, that's pretty much up to you. Do you want to keep playing or do you want some time off?"

"Play," we all said.

Curtis smiled his big smile. "That's what I hoped. I've arranged for someone to be here for your practices, but you older girls are going to have to give her a hand." Her? Who was he talking about?

"Tara can be here every day after school to keep things going," said Curtis. Tara, who had been skating at most of our practices, smiled at us.

"I know I can't coach you like Curtis does," she said quietly, "but with your help, I'm sure we can keep things going until he gets back." There was a moment of silence while we took in this piece of news. Then I said, "Sounds good to me. Thanks, Tara. We need all the help we can get."

"Maybe when I get back, we'll have a game against the Peewee boys," said Curtis. "They've been practicing a bit, but I think if you keep working, you'll give them a good game."

A game! Everyone's eyes lit up. Yes!

The only one who looked a bit worried was Alice. "I'm not sure I'm ready for a game yet," she said quietly.

"Sure you are, Alice," said Sam. We all nodded in agreement.

"You'll be surprised at how well you'll do," said Curtis. "Those boys won't know what hit them."

We should have known that things were going too well. My mom calls it Murphy's Law. On Saturday night, someone trashed the skate-sharpening machine. For as long as I can remember, the sharpening machine had stood in the entranceway to Dave's Gas Bar. It was the only place within three hundred kilometers to get skates sharpened. Sometimes it broke down for a day or two, but Dave was always able to get it up and running again. For a dollar apiece, your skates usually came out sharper than they went in.

According to Dave, a snow machine had pulled up in front of the station around 10:00 PM. He thought it was coming in for gas or something. But instead the driver quickly passed a rope around the skate-sharpening machine and dragged it off the porch and about a kilometer down the road, where it was run over several times. It was toast. Dave told the RCMP it happened so fast that he didn't even realize what was going on until the machine was gone. The driver was dressed in a Darth Vader helmet, so Dave couldn't tell who it was. It could have been anybody. But who?

Fort Desperation gets its share of vandalism, but this was the first time that I had been directly affected. Last summer someone broke most of windows at the school, but this was different. No skate-sharpening machine, no skating. It was simple. Why would someone do something like that?

One bad thing about skating on the pond is that your skates get dull really fast—way faster than in the arena. Without the sharpening machine, our practices were going to end really soon.

Luckily, at school on Monday, the Smithers girls let everyone know that their dad was driving to Hay River the next day and would take all of the skates that we could deliver to the detachment by 9:00 AM. We had a quick practice after school, and then everyone walked by the detachment to drop off their skates.

This solution would work once, but what about next week, and the week after that? Corporal Smithers was really nice about everything. He piled all the skates into two boxes and said he'd let us know how much it cost when he got back in two days. We helped him load the boxes into the back of the huge RCMP SUV, and then asked him if he had any leads.

"Not yet," he said, "but Fort Desperation is a small place and nothing stays a secret forever."

Chapter Eleven

When Corporal Smithers returned to town, he brought not only our skates, but a beat-up old skate-sharpening machine as well.

"A donation from the Hay River Hardware Store," he said, grinning. "They sharpen with a grindstone now, so they had this old-timer stored in the back, waiting for a new home. I'll take it over to the gas station and see if Dave wants it."

ACP. We all grabbed our skates and headed to the pond for a quick skate before dark. It had been three days, the longest any of us had gone without skating since the pond froze.

Six of us arrived together and immediately noticed that there was something on the ice: fluorescent red paint. At first it made no sense, but then Sam put it all together.

"*GIRLS GO HOME*. It says *GIRLS GO HOME*," yelled Sam. "Why would it say that?"

We stood there in stunned silence. This was meant for us. Why would anyone do this?

"Maybe it's a joke," said Sarah.

"I don't think so," replied Alice quietly. "Look at this." She gestured to several holes in the ice. They weren't too deep—maybe three inches or so. Just enough to make skating into them dangerous.

"Looks like they were chopped with an axe."

"Somebody hates us," said Sarah, all of a sudden sounding near tears.

"Well, I don't know about hating us, but they sure don't want us to play hockey," I replied quickly, before she started to cry.

We ran back to the café as fast as we could and almost fell through the door in a heap. All six of us tried explaining to my mom what had happened. Eventually, she got the story straight. Her jaw clenched, and her eyes got very narrow.

"We'll get to the bottom of this," she said in a low, angry voice, as she picked up the phone.

She talked with Corporal Smithers for a few minutes and agreed to meet him at the pond. Back we went with flashlights. Word must have gotten out quickly, because there were already several people at the pond when we got there. Everyone was furious. Corporal Smithers carefully looked over the area and shook his head.

"There are at least a dozen holes as well as the paint," he said quietly to my mom. "Holes like that are really dangerous if a skater doesn't see them."

People kept asking the same two questions. Who would do such a thing? And why?

"If we get the answer to one question, we'll probably get the answer to the other," said Corporal Smithers. "You girls have any idea who wants you to quit playing hockey?"

We all looked at each other and shook our heads.

"We haven't even beaten anybody yet," said Sarah.

"Well," he said, "we'll figure it out. In the meantime, we'll repair the rink. I'll call the fire hall and see if they have a pump we can use tomorrow. If any of you get any bright ideas about this, come and tell me.

Don't try to do anything on your own." When he said this, he looked hard at us girls, to make sure we were really listening. We all nodded.

Sam's eyes suddenly went wide. "Do you think this has anything to do with the skate sharpener?" she asked him.

"Good question. Hard to say right now, but I'll keep it in mind. Okay everyone, time to go home. We'll get to work on this tomorrow. You girls won't miss any more practices."

We walked home in silence. In a small place like Fort Desperation, everybody pretty well knew everybody else. I wondered who could have done this, and why? We're nice girls. What had we done to make somebody so mad at us?

It was the main topic of conversation at school the next day. At lunch we narrowed down the field of suspects. It had to have been a male, probably young, maybe with a Ski-Doo. That only left about two hundred suspects. No problem!

"Maybe we should set a trap," suggested Opal. In addition to figure skating, Opal read mysteries—lots of them.

"You heard what the corporal said, Opal. We're not supposed to try anything on our own," replied Geraldine.

"But it's not like we're dealing with a vicious criminal or anything. It's probably some goofy hockey player who's scared of the competition," said Opal.

"A hockey player wouldn't have trashed the skate sharpener," added Sam quietly.

"That's true," I said. "But do we really know that the two incidents are related?"

"So, do we just wait and hope that it doesn't happen again?" asked Opal in an irritated voice.

"I guess so," said Sam. "Maybe whoever did it will get bored with the idea and go away."

We all nodded in agreement. We would keep our fingers crossed.

Chapter Twelve

After school, we all met at the pond to find the ice surface freshly flooded. The head of the volunteer fire department, Len, was just putting away his hoses when we arrived.

"Wow, that's great," we exclaimed. "It's even better than it was before!"

"Thanks. It was a good excuse to get out of the office," Len admitted. "I even painted some lines on before I flooded it. Scraped off most of the message too."

We now actually had three lines across the rink: a red center line with a wobbly face-off circle in the middle and a blue line halfway to each net. What a concept. Now the new girls would get to learn about offsides! The nasty message was very faint and impossible to read, and the holes were all gone. Our rink was better than ever.

"Maybe we should thank the idiot who made all of this possible," laughed Ger.

"We will. When we catch him," responded Opal.

Len laughed and finished putting away his equipment. "There were Ski-Doo tracks beside most of the holes," he said, "so I'd guess whoever did it doesn't like to get too far from his machine."

"A clue!" shouted Opal. She wasn't going to give up on the whole sleuthing angle any time soon.

We had good practices for the next couple of days, except that Alice wasn't there. I wasn't exactly worried, but it was kind of strange. She never missed practice. I hadn't even seen her at school. Finally I asked Michael where she was.

"She's stayed home the past few days. She broke up with her jerky boyfriend on the weekend, and he keeps hassling her."

"Oh, that's not good," I replied, as if I really knew about these things.

"She figures he'll calm down when he realizes she really means it, but in the meantime, she's staying out of his way."

"She should come to hockey. We'd protect her."

"Sure you would," he laughed. "I don't think he's dangerous, but he is an idiot. All he thinks about is his snow machine."

"Kind of like us and hockey?"

"No way. Hockey is important. I mean it's real…"

"Yeah, you're right. Hockey is important. Have you heard anything about the arena?"

"They're saying early December. Hope they're right. It's getting too cold to play outside."

Michael was right. It was dipping down to minus thirty at night and not warming up too much during the daytime. At least the skies were blue and clear, making the days seem a little longer. Someone had dumped off some firewood at the pond, so we sometimes had a bonfire going at practices. It gave us a way to warm up our fingers and toes a bit. Tara was doing a good job of keeping the practices going, but we were all anxious to get into the arena.

Friday morning was warmer and cloudy, with soft snow falling. According to the weather report on the radio, it was going to warm up for a few days. I got an urgent note from Opal in math. It said *Get everyone together for an important meeting in the lunchroom.* I had no idea what it was about, but I passed the note around. At noon, most of the team met at a table in the back corner.

"What's so important?" asked Sam.

"I have an idea," said Opal. Her sister nodded in agreement. "Since today is Friday and it's warming up, I thought maybe the Hockey Vandal might be getting ready to strike again. I think we should set a trap."

There was a long silence. A trap? Us? Everyone began to talk at once.

"Corporal Smithers told us to bring our ideas to him, and not to do anything on our own," said Ger.

"Yeah. Dad would be furious if we tried anything," added Daisy. Her sisters nodded.

"Well," said Opal, "maybe you three shouldn't be involved, but the rest of us could just sort of hang out at the pond tonight after dark and see if he shows up."

"We'll just freeze for nothing," said Sam.

"Maybe, maybe not," replied Opal. "It's worth a try. Say for an hour or so after everyone goes home."

"What are we going to do if he does show up?" asked Sam. "Beat him with our hockey sticks?"

There was a long silence while we thought about that one. I, for one, was definitely not into violence.

I had a brainwave. Without thinking, I blurted it out. "I know. We could take his picture."

"Yeah," said Opal with enthusiasm. "We've got a new digital camera."

"So do we," added several other excited voices. "We could all bring cameras, with flashes on them, and take a whole bunch of pictures at once. Then we'd run away." Oh boy. Was this a bright idea, or a really stupid one? I wasn't sure.

"Let's vote," said Opal, obviously totally keen on the idea. "Who's in favor?" Seven hands shot up.

"Who's against?" Four hands...the Smithers girls and Ger.

"Jess, you didn't vote," said Sam.

"This is all happening too fast for me. I'm still thinking about it." It's not that I'm a chicken or anything, but I really don't like jumping into things without thinking a bit first. I'm like my dad that way.

"Well, whatever," said Opal, with a flip of her chin. "Seven of us are ready to go. But we have to keep this secret. No telling anyone." We all nodded in agreement.

Daisy, who had been looking very unhappy, said, "After you take the pictures, you can bring them to our house, and we'll download them onto the computer. We really can't go to the pond with you, but I don't think Dad would be too mad if we just printed the pictures."

Sam looked at me for a moment, and then said, "I think it's a good idea. You should come."

I sighed. "Yeah, okay. I'll come."

It was agreed. We'd go to the pond after supper for a skate and then, after everyone else left, we'd hide behind the snowbank and wait one hour, no longer. Everyone would bring some kind of camera.

"Don't forget to wear warm clothes," said Sam as we headed off to classes. Oh boy, I thought, what are we getting ourselves into?

Chapter Thirteen

"Mom, can I borrow the digital camera tonight?" I asked innocently when I got home from school. She was going to ground me forever when this was all over…if I was still alive to ground.

"Sure, honey. It's on my desk," she replied from the kitchen. The café was quiet, as it usually is at that time of the afternoon. It gave her an hour or two to get the supper menu ready. We had about a dozen or so regulars for supper every night and sometimes a few travelers. Being Friday night, there might even be a family or two.

I unloaded the dishwasher and tidied up the tables in front. Mom likes to do the cooking and prep work herself, so there really wasn't much more I could do.

I couldn't stop worrying about tonight. If only I could talk to Mom about it. But there was no way. She'd put a stop to the whole thing right away, and that would not do a lot for my popularity on the team. Besides, it wasn't very likely that the Hockey Vandal would show up at the pond again. Most likely, we'd just get very cold for nothing.

After supper we met at the pond and skated around, waiting. I brought Spider along for moral support. Spider isn't much of a guard dog, but he is big. One of the strangest things about Spider is that he's afraid of ice. That's actually a good thing, because it means I can bring him to the pond when we play hockey, and he stays off the rink. He runs round and round the edge, whining, but at least he doesn't steal the puck.

Soft snowflakes were still drifting down, but enough people had shoveled when they arrived to keep the ice fairly clean. Someone had lit a big bonfire, and groups of little kids were zooming around, screaming and chasing each other. The generator was going, so our floodlight was on. Normally this was one of my favorite things to do, but tonight I couldn't enjoy it. My stomach was in a knot, and my whole body was tense.

In all there were eight of us on the ice. Sam, Opal and Ruby were definitely the ringleaders tonight. They were excited. They decided that the best place for us to wait was behind the snowbanks on the far side of the rink. The snowbanks were pretty high now, so we'd be invisible from the ice itself. Behind them, the bush was thick. It wouldn't be too hard to disappear into it if we had to. At about 9:00 PM the owner of the generator shut it down and loaded it into his truck. A few kids continued to skate in the dark, but fairly soon they too took off their skates and went home. The eight of us skated over to the bench and removed our skates. All of a sudden, it seemed very quiet and isolated.

"I wore extra socks," said Opal, "and my neck warmer."

"It's a good thing it's not too cold tonight," added Sam.

"A perfect night for vandalism," said Ruby, with a wicked grin.

We trooped across the deserted rink and stationed ourselves behind the snowbanks. Spider settled down beside me with an eager expression on his face that said, "Now what?" The moon was covered by clouds, but the outlines of the rink and the bush were very easy to see. At either end of the rink, homemade wooden goal nets stood on guard, while three benches lined the side closest to the road. The coals from the bonfire still glowed. In the winter, we're pretty slack about putting out fires. They're pretty much left to take care of themselves.

We pulled out our cameras and got them ready. Sam and Opal had brought flashlights, which were very helpful. There were five digital cameras and three film cameras.

"This camera hasn't been used since last Christmas," said Ruby, holding up a little point-and-shoot. "It will be fun to see what's on the film."

"So what are we going to do if this guy actually shows up?" I finally asked.

"Well, I guess we should wait to see if he's really going to do something bad, and then, on a signal, we should all stand up and take a picture at the same time," said Opal.

"Yeah. And then we run."

"In eight different directions."

"We'll meet at the Smithers' house."

Everyone was throwing out ideas. To pass the time, we all tried to guess who the vandal could be. The suggestions got pretty bizarre. Someone even suggested Joe, the hockey coach for the boys, because he didn't want us to humiliate his teams. It was past nine thirty, and we were starting to feel the cold. Ski-Doos could be heard in the distance, but nothing seemed to be coming this way.

"I wish we had a thermos of hot chocolate," said Ruby. "Yeah," agreed Opal. "On our next stakeout, we'll have to remember hot chocolate."

"Listen," said Sam in a loud whisper.

Slowly, the sound of a Ski-Doo got closer and louder. It was coming from the trails behind the school. Suddenly, a headlight came into view through the trees. We held our breath and watched intently. The machine was traveling slowly, approaching the rink from one end. It stopped for a moment while the driver seemed to look around, and then crept ahead until it came to a stop beside the glowing firepit. The driver shut the motor off and just sat there, very still. We froze in our places. He pulled off his helmet and looked around without leaving his machine.

It was too dark to see his face, but he looked big. My heart was hammering like a drum. Surely he could hear it. I looked sideways at Sam and the others. Their breath was coming out in tiny streams. Nobody moved a muscle, not even Spider.

Finally the guy on the Ski-Doo seemed to relax. He placed his helmet on the ground and pulled something from the carrier behind his seat. An axe! He walked slowly over to the closest goal net, not far from the firepit. He looked around once more and then swung the axe. The left side of the goal crumpled to the ice. He swung at the other side, smashing it to the ice as well. Then he started to drag the mangled carcass toward the firepit. He poked at the glowing fire with his boot, stirring it up and getting a small flame going. Then he lifted the goal and tossed it onto the fire. With new fuel, the fire flared up again quickly. Behind the snowbank, we all tensed. How long should we wait? Should we really do this, or just stay hidden until he left?

"On three," came a whisper from Sam. "Pass it on." I turned to Alyssa on my right and passed the message.

"One, two, three," came a loud whisper from down the line. We all stood up, cameras raised.

"Hey, you!" shouted Opal.

The Vandal turned toward us and froze. Camera flashes started going off, one after the other.

"What the—" He stood up and stared, stunned for a moment, it seemed. We stood and stared too. For a moment everything was still. Deep in the bush, an owl hooted. Then the Vandal was all motion. He turned and jumped onto the Ski-Doo, cranked its motor into action and was gone in a roar and a cloud of snow, across the rink and down the trail.

We all jumped up and down and hollered. High fives all around.

"Let's get out of here fast, before he comes back," said Sam.

We ran across the rink to the firepit, where our goal was engulfed in flames. I took a few photos of it, just for good measure.

"Hey, he left his helmet and the axe. I'll bring them," said Ruby.

Then we hit the road, running as fast as we possibly could, our skates slung over our shoulders. Spider was so excited that he kept jumping up on everyone and nipping at our heels. It only took about five minutes to get to the Smithers' house, but it seemed like hours.

We kept watching over our shoulders, ears tuned for the sound of a solitary Ski-Doo. We charged onto the Smithers' front porch and knocked hard.

"Everyone here?" asked Sam. A quick head count revealed all eight of us. Daisy opened the door, and we piled in. Everyone was talking at once. I sank to the floor in relief. My legs felt like rubber.

"That was really scary," I said to Sam when I was able to speak.

"Yeah. That axe made me think twice about the plan."

"Not me," replied Opal. "I knew we could do it." There was silence while we thought about what could have happened. But we had survived, and our plan had worked. We had evidence!

Chapter Fourteen

We piled into the living room, where a computer sat on a desk in the corner. The five digital cameras came out of our pockets and onto the desk beside the computer. We'd keep the film for backup if the digital photos didn't turn out.

"This could take a while," said Daisy. "Let's start with this one," she said, taking Sam's camera. She plugged a cord into the camera and then the computer, and clicked on a few icons. "It's downloading. How many shots did you take?"

"Two or three, I think," replied Sam.

"Okay. Here they are." Three small photos appeared on the screen. The fire was bright in the background, and in front was a dark figure. How would we ever be able to tell who it was?

"I'll blow them up a bit," said Daisy, who obviously knew what she was doing. "All those media studies classes are finally paying off," she said, grinning. "This looks like the best one. I'll work on it first."

She zeroed in on the mysterious head, clicked the mouse a few times, and we watched the head grow. A few more clicks, and it became lighter.

"Anyone you know?" We all jostled closer for a better look.

"He looks sort of familiar. A bit like...Cory. Alice's boyfriend. Ex-boyfriend, I mean," said Sam. We looked closer.

"Yeah...maybe. It's hard to really see. Can we look at another one?"

So we looked at several more. It wasn't until the third camera that we got the shot that left no doubt. It was Cory, all right! Alyssa, who had taken the photo, was very proud. "I used the zoom," she explained, "and set the speed at eight hundred, for night shots."

The photo showed Cory clearly, mouth open, eyes wide, caught in the act with the axe in his hand and the burning goal beside him. Wow!

"Why would Cory be a vandal?" asked Alyssa. "I mean, what did we ever do to him?"

I explained what Michael had told me about Cory not wanting Alice to play hockey. It seemed like a pretty lame reason for what he had done. "I just don't get this whole boyfriend thing," I said. "It seems like most of the girls with boyfriends spend their time fighting and breaking up. I mean, what's the point?"

Everyone else nodded in agreement. What did we know about the world of boyfriends?

"I'll make some prints of this one and a few others for backup," said Daisy, springing into action again. It was getting late, so we all took turns calling home to let our parents know where we were. By midnight, we had four good prints, and we were exhausted.

"Well, this should do it," said Daisy. "I guess we'll have to show these to Dad. How about if we wait till the morning?" We all agreed. There was a honk outside. My mom was here to pick us up. All eight of us managed to pile into the truck, both front and back. Spider got to run behind. Weary good nights hung in the darkness as we staggered into our houses.

I managed not to tell Mom what we had done, although it was hard, but I figured she'd find out soon enough. Then I'd be in trouble. Maybe Corporal Smithers would arrest us for not listening to him. Was there a law against ignoring RCMP advice?

At 9:00 AM, Daisy phoned. "We should do this pretty soon. Dad's gone to the detachment for the morning, so we'd better catch him there before something else comes up." We decided to phone everyone and have them meet at her house so we could walk to the detachment together. By 10:00 AM, we were ready to go. Opal was carrying the helmet and axe, while Daisy had an important-looking brown envelope of photos. We were all quiet.

"I'm more nervous about this than about our stakeout," said Ruby. "What do you think he's going to do to us?"

"Hard to say," replied Daisy. "He might be proud of you, or he might be furious. Depends on how much danger he thinks you put yourselves in, I guess."

We all crowded into the detachment entryway, where we were greeted by a young constable.

"Hi, girls. What are you doing out so early on a Saturday morning?"

"We're here to see my dad," said Daisy. Her sisters nodded behind her.

"Okay. Just wait a sec while I see if he's busy."

We could hear a muffled conversation down the hall, followed by Corporal Smithers' appearance.

"To what do I owe this honor, ladies?" he asked, eyeing us carefully.

Daisy handed him the envelope silently.

"We took these photos last night at the rink, sir," said Sam, in quick explanation. "Your girls weren't there. Daisy just printed them for us."

Before he opened the envelope, he stared at each of us in turn. We all smiled bravely, trying to look like confident sleuths. He pulled out the photos and examined each one before saying anything.

"Is this what I think it is?" he asked quietly. We nodded.

"Here's his helmet too, and his axe. He left them behind when he ran away." Opal proudly handed the black helmet and well-used axe to him. She was the only one who didn't seem worried about what his reaction was going to be. Maybe she really was a sleuth.

"You girls had better come into my office and explain this from the beginning," he said. We crowded into his office, and I led things off. The story came out kind of confused, but he got the idea. He kept looking at us very seriously. Finally he spoke. "Do you girls remember what I told you after that last incident?"

Silence.

"Well?"

"Yes, sir," I finally said. Everyone nodded in agreement.

"But we didn't really think anyone would show up," said Opal quickly. "It was really just a theory we were testing." Wow. Testing a theory? Where did that come from? Opal really read too much.

"Did any of you think about what might have happened if he had decided to go after you instead of running away?"

"We were going to run into the bush in eight different directions," said Opal, confident that her plan would impress him.

"So maybe he would only have caught one or two of you? And then what?" Dead silence. He heaved a long sigh and shook his head.

"Well, you girls are going to have some explaining to do to your parents before this is through." He paused. "But first," he said as he held up the photos, "this young man has some explaining to do to me. I'm going to have a look at the crime scene. Please go home and stay there until you hear otherwise. You're all grounded."

We trooped out the door.

"Grounded by the RCMP. Wow! That's a new one," said Opal proudly. Nothing seemed to faze Opal.

Chapter Fifteen

Since it was Saturday morning, the café was really busy. All of the tables and most of the counter seats were full. The next few hours flew by while I served, made coffee and cleaned up. I tried my best to smile, like a good waitress should, but it was hard. Let's just say my mind wasn't on my job. Finally, after the lunch rush, Mom and I had time to sit down and have a sandwich.

"Going to the rink this afternoon?" she asked, between bites of her BLT.

"No."

There was a long pause.

"Something wrong?"

"Yeah. Kind of. Actually, it's not all bad. We caught the Hockey Vandal last night, or at least we took photos of him."

"What?" Mom locked her eagle eyes on me. I squirmed. Then I told her the whole story. When I was done, I waited for the explosion. Finally she just shook her head and said, "You girls."

That was it? Of course not. But at least there hadn't been an explosion.

"Reg is right, you know." Reg was Daisy's dad. "You could have gotten hurt. And you should have taken the plan to him instead of going ahead with it on your own."

"I know, Mom, but it seemed like such a goofy idea. I don't think anybody but Opal thought that he'd actually show up. Actually, it's kind of cool how it worked out."

"Well, I'll be interested to hear how Reg's talk with Cory goes. I expect we'll hear about it soon."

No sooner had she spoken than the phone rang. Mom answered it and had a conversation that consisted mainly of "Yup," "Uh-huh" and "Okay."

"That was Reg. He wants us all to come to the detachment at three this afternoon."

I gulped.

I finished cleaning up while Mom prepared some moose stew for supper. At five to three, we hung the *Back Soon* sign in the window of the café and headed to the detachment. Inside, it was already crowded. The room really wasn't built to hold twenty people, but we all squeezed in. Corporal Smithers came out of his office, looking serious.

"Thanks for coming. Sorry there's nowhere to sit, but this won't take long. I hope your girls have told you why we're here." He paused, and everyone nodded. "Well, the short story is that I followed up on their detective work and interviewed the young man in the photos. I also returned his helmet and axe. He admitted to the whole thing, including the paint incident and trashing the skate sharpener."

"All right," said Opal, high-fiving her sister. All eight of us were grinning now. We had actually caught the right person. The parents were all talking at once. The hubbub was pretty loud. Finally the corporal spoke up again.

"I'd like to thank the girls for their help, but I'd also like to warn them that in the future, they should leave the policing of Fort Desperation to the RCMP. Luckily, this young man is not a violent sort. In fact, he's pretty embarrassed right now. But if it had been another type of person, the whole story might have turned out very differently. So that's about it. Cory will probably be charged with mischief and made to pay for the skate sharpener. That's up to the courts, I guess. I think it's safe to say that the case of the Hockey Vandal is closed. If you want to see the photos, they're right here. Thanks for coming."

With that, he held out the photos to the closest parents. Everyone wanted to see them while we explained in gory detail, to everyone, all at once, just what had happened. It was all okay. We weren't arrested. In fact, we were sort of heroes. Wow!

Sam was grinning from ear to ear. "I was kind of worried that we were going to be in big trouble."

"Me too," I said. "Hey, want to go skate for a while? I think Curtis comes back tomorrow. I've got a few moves I'd like to work on."

We all headed home to get our skates. Within half an hour, most of us had made it to the pond. It was already getting dark, but that didn't matter. The pond was ours again. The only reminder of the case of the Hockey Vandal was the remains of the goal, which still lay in the firepit beside the ice.

"My dad said he'd make another one," said Opal as she stood looking at the ruined net. "Might even be ready by the time Curtis gets back. Boy, are we going to have a story to tell him."

Chapter Sixteen

Curtis came back on schedule, and he was pretty impressed with our detective work, but he didn't let it get in the way of our practices. With lines on our rink, we actually got to teach the new players the strategies of the game. We got better with every practice, and by the time the arena finally opened two weeks before Christmas, we were beginning to feel like a team. Sam, Geraldine and I were so busy with the team that we didn't even have much time to play with the boys, whose hearts weren't exactly broken.

As he promised, Curtis got us some games with the Peewees. The first game was a disaster. We must have set some sort of record for the most offsides in one game. After the first period, the scorekeeper stopped posting the score. Alice must have stopped a hundred shots, but quite a few got past her. Curtis wouldn't let us get depressed about it. In fact, we had a lot of fun. We laughed a lot and after the game, the Peewee coach, Joe, said he had never seen such a polite team. He told us that we really didn't have to apologize if we bumped into someone. We're still working on that.

During the Christmas holidays, we really started to come together. New hockey equipment had turned up under most of our Christmas trees, so we were even beginning to look like hockey players. I got a great pair of new skates, size eights, and some bright pink stick tape. Everyone was figuring out how to play their positions, and more and more often, the newer girls were carrying the puck and making plays. Opal and Ruby on defense were awesome. They worked together perfectly and nobody could get by them with a puck anymore. But the real star was Alice. She was unbelievable. Now that she was used to the heavy equipment, she was like Superwoman. All those years of stopping soccer balls had paid off. She never said a single word about Cory. Maybe she was too embarrassed. Although she was older than us and a major soccer hero, Alice was pretty shy and not at all stuck up. If she didn't want to talk about Cory, that was fine with us. In the dressing room, we showed off our new bruises, and Sam brought a CD player so that we could play really loud music to get us pumped up.

Fort Desperation's community arena is really old. According to local legend, it was built in the 1950s beside the old residential school, which housed three hundred students from up and down the river. The school is long gone, but the arena is still standing. It's a long Quonset hut that looks a bit like an oil drum cut in half lengthwise. An old trailer attached to one side houses the two dressing rooms. They're incredibly cold, even with the extra electric heaters going, but for us girls, just getting a whole dressing room to ourselves was a major step forward.

After Christmas, a special hockey night was announced, with games starting at four o'clock and going till midnight. The snack bar would be up and running, with hot dogs, pop and other assorted health foods. The whole lobby was decorated for the event with people's rejected Christmas decorations: old strings of lights with big bulbs, those long twisty ropes of tinsel and unmatched faded ornaments. Christmas carols crackled over the PA system, even at our practices.

The games were arranged according to age, and our team was going to play the Peewee boys team at 5:30 PM. We were nervous. It was our first game in public, and we were desperate not to get blown out of the arena.

We all got to the arena good and early so we'd have time to do our stretches and other professional stuff like retaping our sticks. After we were dressed, Curtis came into the dressing room to give us a little pep talk. Tara, who was now our official assistant coach, came too.

"Well, are you ready for this?" he asked. We stayed quiet. This was going to be embarrassing. We could just feel it in our bones. We knew that the arena was starting to fill up out there. What if they laughed at us?

"This is your chance to show your families just how far you've come," he continued. "Just think back two months, to when you started this team, and how much better you are today. If you skate hard and play your best game, you'll do fine. Those boys are a bit cocky. I think you're going to surprise them."

Finally, Opal broke the silence. "I'd really like to beat them. They are so arrogant. They deserve to lose," she said emphatically.

"Yeah, I'm tired of losing to those little squirts," added Daisy. "You know, I think we really could beat them if we had just a small miracle. Just a small one."

"Well, ladies, let's go find our miracle," said Curtis with a pump of his fist.

"Yeah," we all yelled, as loud as we could.

Chapter Seventeen

We filed slowly onto the ice and eyed the stands. There were a lot of people up there...probably a hundred or so. My mom was waving and smiling, and Mrs. Smithers had started chanting, "Go girls go." Oh, this was so embarrassing.

We ran through some shooting drills to get Alice warmed up. When the ref came on the ice, Curtis whistled us over to the bench. He was smiling from ear to ear.

"Well, girls, maybe we'll get our miracle." We looked at each other and then back at him.

"How?" I asked.

"How many of you are here today?" Curtis asked.

We started counting.

"Fourteen," Alice said

"Take a look at their bench." We all turned and looked. There weren't very many of them. In fact, a quick count came up with eight, including the goalie. Smiles started to spread across our faces. Only seven skaters. If we played our cards right, we might wear them out.

"You can do this, girls," said Curtis. "Just skate their legs off."

We hit the ice. We were so nervous the first few shifts that we couldn't do anything right. Opal gave the puck away right in front of our net, and despite Alice's desperate leap, the score was 1–0 within the first minute. Then I lost the face-off, Sam tripped, Ruby and Opal collided and it was 2–0. This was going to be even worse than we thought. The stands were already quiet, except for Mrs. Smithers, who kept yelling, "Go, girls," at every opportunity.

But after a few shifts we started to settle down. Sam, Geraldine and I started passing the puck around, just like in practice, waiting for a good opportunity to take a shot. The Peewees were zooming everywhere, just trying to get their sticks on the puck. Opal and Ruby were solid on defense, and the boys couldn't seem to get around them. Finally, at the end of the first period, Daisy intercepted the puck at center ice, and quickly passed it to Michelle, who flipped it over the sprawling goalie. It was in. We mobbed Michelle. In the stands, our parents went wild, just like we'd won the Stanley Cup or something. Curtis was grinning ear to ear.

During the break between periods, while the PA system pumped out loud rock music, Curtis gave us a real pep talk. It really was possible that we could take this game. We listened to everything he said with new enthusiasm. The trick was to keep our shifts short, so that we were always fresh and skating our hardest. We had enough players that we could actually get a bit rested between shifts. We hit the ice with a loud cheer.

The second period was tough. Those little guys were in good shape, and they weren't going to give up any time soon. Since they were playing girls, there was no bodychecking allowed, but they were getting a bit desperate. Their biggest player, Josh Simpson, nailed Sam as she reached for the puck. Josh got a three-minute penalty for bodychecking. Sam was really slow getting up and skating to the bench.

"Are you okay?" I asked.

"Oh yeah. I've had worse. It's just that I wasn't expecting it. I'm kind of getting used to not having to worry about body checks, you know?"

"I know what you mean. It sort of makes me want to go out and check back, but the last thing we need now is a penalty."

We had worked on power plays a bit in our last practice. The Smithers girls made up the offensive line, while Opal and Ruby stayed on defense. We took the puck straight into their zone and set up a passing pattern with Michelle, who was the biggest and strongest, in front of their net. After about a solid minute of passing, Ruby sent the puck across to Fancy, who fired it at the net. Michelle stuck out her stick and tipped it up into the air, over the goalie's glove. It was 2–2!

The crowd erupted in cheers. By now, all of our families were sitting together and getting kind of rowdy. The little Beaulieu kids were waving a piece of cardboard with "Go girls" written on it. Not too original, but that was okay. One by one they started clapping until they were all in unison, clapping and stomping and hollering. Wow. It was all for us!

Between the second and third periods there was a longer break so that the Zamboni could clean the ice.

This was really big time. We went to the dressing room and flopped on the benches. I looked around as everyone took off their helmets. Hair was dripping wet, faces red. There was no doubt about it, we were playing hard.

The door burst open, and Mrs. Smithers and my mom came in with a tray of cut-up oranges. We grabbed them thirstily. "Way to go, girls. You're awesome," said Mrs. Smithers. We were all talking at once, eating oranges and laughing. Curtis and Tara walked into the dressing room too.

"Okay, girls, settle down. This isn't over yet. Those boys don't want to lose, so you're going to have to keep up the pressure. Can you do it?"

The room erupted in a loud roar. Can we do it? Of course we could. We left the room feeling much different than we had an hour before.

The boys started the third period with a huge burst of energy. Their center slipped around our defense and raced in alone on Alice. He deked left and tried to tuck a backhand past her. Alice did the splits and trapped the puck under her pad. What a save! The crowd went wild again.

Back and forth we went. The boys were tired, but they sure weren't going to give up. With less than a minute to go, Sarah snuck around Trevor, their last defenseman, and headed toward the net. Knowing he was beaten, Trevor stuck out his stick and tripped her. Sarah fell flat on her face, the puck slowly gliding into the goalie's glove. The referee's shrill whistle sounded almost before Sarah hit the ice.

"Penalty shot," chanted the crowd. "Penalty shot." Sarah got slowly to her feet and looked at the referee. As Trevor headed to the penalty box, the ref called Sarah over and talked to her. Then they skated together to center ice and he put the puck down. Curtis signaled a time out to the ref. We all headed over to the bench and made room for Sarah in front of Curtis.

"Penalty shot," she said, looking absolutely terrified.

"That's great, Sarah. Don't worry. I know you can beat him. He's weak on his stick side. Have you noticed that?"

Sarah shook her head slowly. She was one of our youngest and smallest players. For her age, she was probably also our best player. She seemed to have a knack for sneaking and stickhandling around much bigger players, and, although she didn't shoot very hard, she was pretty accurate.

Curtis smiled gently at his little niece. "Take a deep breath and then stare at the goalie for a while, just to make him more nervous. Take your time, and go when you're ready. There's no rush. Try to raise it high on his stick side. He'll probably go down, thinking you can't raise it, so you'll just have to fool him. Can you do that?" With a weak smile, she nodded her head and slowly turned and skated, all alone, to center ice. We all stood along the boards by the bench, watching and waiting. She looked so small. The crowd was dead quiet.

Sarah stood at center ice, staring at the goalie for what seemed a very long time. Then, she stood up a little straighter, looked down at the puck, up again at the goalie and started to skate. She took the puck with her stick and began to pick up speed. She never took her eyes off the goalie.

It all seemed to happen in slow motion. Sarah headed to the right, swerved suddenly to the left and then at the last second pivoted back to the right and fired a shot, right into the top corner of the net.

She threw her arms into the air, and we mobbed her. The crowd went wild. The Peewee goalie slammed his stick against the goalpost. The score was 3–2 with forty-three seconds to go.

Sarah skated wildly to the bench and threw herself at Curtis.

"Uncle, Uncle, I did like you said. I did like you said."

Curtis gave her a big hug. "You sure did, Sarah. It was perfect."

My line was on now. The Peewees dumped the puck into our end and pulled their goalie. They were going with six skaters. Desperation time. They were moving the puck quickly, trying to set up for a good shot. Alice fended off two weak shots, and then Opal snagged a rebound and started moving. I headed down the ice as fast as I could skate, looking back quickly and calling her name. She saw me and fired the puck to center ice.

The two defenders were moving fast too, and they came at me one on each side as I snagged the pass. I think we kind of had a three-way collision at the blue line. Anyway, we all went down in a pile. Funny thing was, I guess I pushed the puck as I fell. It just kept going, slowly, toward the net. Everyone was screaming

"The puck, the puck!" The crowd was on its feet, roaring. The defensemen scrambled up and took off after it, but they were too late. The puck sort of dribbled into the net and the buzzer went. It was over.

Our whole team roared onto the ice and jumped on me. I thought I was going to suffocate. Then we all went and jumped on Alice till she screamed to let her up. In the stands, our families were just about as happy, but I don't think anyone got piled on. We shook hands, and Joe, the other coach, congratulated us on a hard-fought game. We were pretty proud. We had had our little miracle.

Chapter Eighteen

Everyone went to the café after the game for a celebration, and Curtis ordered "hot chocolate for the house." He'd seemed much happier lately. We liked to think it was because of us, but actually, I think it was because of Tara. They were spending a lot of time together, even away from the arena.

"Ladies. I have an announcement. Listen up." Curtis stood on a chair at the counter so he could see everyone. "We've found a girls' tournament to go to, if you're interested." If we were interested! Who was he kidding? We burst into applause. A road trip! It's what we had dreamed of, right from the start.

"Grande Prairie is hosting a girl's tourney in February, and they have a mixed-age category that would fit us perfectly. Interested?" We cheered and carried on for a few minutes. Grande Prairie. Not exactly Edmonton, but what the heck. It had a movie theater, a swimming pool, a shopping mall and restaurants. It would be great.

"Okay. Well, I'll take that as a 'yes.' We'll have to do a bit of fund-raising. A few of the mothers have agreed to organize a bus, but you'll have to come up with some money for hotel rooms and meals."

After that, we really got serious. We practiced every day after school and played two games a week against the Peewees. The scores were getting closer all the time, even when we had the same number of players. We were even starting to talk about challenging the Bantams, but that could wait until after Grande Prairie.

When Curtis was away, Tara ran things and did a really good job. She had certainly learned a lot about hockey in a few months. We held two bingo nights in the community hall and raised almost two thousand dollars. We also had a bake sale at the church and were busy selling raffle tickets wherever we could. First prize was two hundred dollars worth of free gas from Dave's Gas Bar. Dave had become our number-one fan. Cory had to work for him after school until the sharpening machine was paid for, and it turned out that he was a good worker, so Dave had hired him permanently. I began to think that maybe Cory wasn't quite as bad a guy as we had thought. I mean, he had to have a few good qualities for someone as great as Alice to go out with him, right?

The week before our big trip, Curtis, Dave and Cory came into our dressing room before practice, carrying three large boxes.

"Ladies, we've got something special for you," Curtis said. Dave broke open a box and pulled out something red. A hockey jersey. "Hope you like them," said Dave, holding one up. "If you're going to a tournament, we figured you needed to look good."

The front of the jersey read *Dave's Gas Bar Super Sleuths*. In the middle was a magnifying glass like

Sherlock Holmes used. On the back was the number 8 and the name *Middleton*. "Guess this one's yours, Jess," Dave said, handing it to me. I was speechless. It was beautiful.

When we finally calmed down, Sam had the brains to say, "Thanks, Dave."

"Oh, don't thank me. Cory had a lot to do with this too. It was his idea, and he helped pay for them."

We were stunned. Cory?

Cory looked really embarrassed, but finally he spoke up.

"I just wanted to say I'm sorry for scaring you. I shouldn't have done that. I was being really stupid." He paused. "Alice…" We all turned to stare at poor Alice, who was suddenly very pale. "I'm really sorry. For everything." Then he grinned. "Anyway, good luck in Grande Prairie. You're going to kick butt." He turned and walked out the door.

We were all quiet for a minute. Nobody knew quite what to say. Then Tara, who had been digging around in the box, held out a jersey to Alice and said, "Here you go." Alice's face brightened as she held up the jersey and admired the big number 1 on the back.

"Cool," she said.

At our last practice before Grande Prairie, Curtis said it was time to pick our team captain and two assistant captains. He explained that the captain should be someone with good leadership skills who would stay calm under pressure. The captain was the only person on the team allowed to talk to the ref if there were any questions on the ice. Curtis thought that we were old enough to pick our own captain and assistants, so he handed out little pieces of paper and pencils to everyone so we could write the name of the player we thought would make the best captain. I voted for Sam.

After the practice, Curtis and Tara came into the dressing room for a quick last-minute talk about the tournament and what to expect. There were five teams entered in our division. It would be a pretty high level of hockey, but he said we were ready for it.

In his hand, he held three pieces of black cloth... a capital C and two capital As. With a big smile, he handed the C to me and said, "You'd better sew this on your jersey before we leave, Jess." I was the captain! Everyone cheered loudly, and then he handed the

As to Sam and Daisy. More cheering. I couldn't believe it. I'd never been the captain of anything before, but I knew I could do it, especially with Sam and Daisy for backup.

So here we are, on the bus. It's almost full, what with fifteen players, two coaches and about twenty chaperones, who say they're coming to cheer us on. I think a lot of them are more interested in shopping than hockey, but what the heck. It's going to be great. It might be minus forty outside, but inside the bus the heater is blasting and it's cozy. We've got our blankets, pillows, junk food, Mp3 players and great movies for the DVD player. In twelve hours we'll be in Grande Prairie. We don't really know what to expect, but that's okay. We'll deal with it. Just a few months ago, this was only a dream, and now it's really happening. The Fort Desperation Super Sleuths are going places, so look out, world!

Fran Hurcomb arrived in the Northwest Territories in 1975 and immediately succumbed to the spell of the North. She lived on a trapline, ran sled dogs for almost twenty years, built and lived on a houseboat and has been a professional photographer for over twenty years. Her first children's book was published in 1999, followed by two northern pictorial histories. Fran lives in Yellowknife with her husband, hockey-playing daughter and several pets.